The Saturday Club

THE BIG ROCK TAKEOVER

*For all good readers at Keble School
and Harold Wood School – JNH*

Text copyright © Jana Novotny Hunter 1998
Illustrations copyright @ Sue Porter 1998

First published in Great Britain in 1998
by Macdonald Young Books
61 Western Road
Hove
East Sussex
BN3 1JD

Photoset in Dorset
by Dorchester Typesetting Group Ltd
Printed and bound in Guernsey
by The Guernsey Press Co. Ltd

ISBN: 0 7500 2249 3

THE BIG ROCK TAKEOVER

•

Jana Novotny Hunter

MACDONALD YOUNG BOOKS

The Saturday Club

1

IT BELONGS TO US

2

THE BIG ROCK TAKEOVER

3

CARNIVAL TIME!

4

THE MONSTER TRAIL

Contents

Contents

•1•

THE GREAT ESCAPE

"It's escaped!" my brother Billy is
yelling at the top of his voice.
"Help, Max, help!"

"I'm coming!"

I burst into the room and trip over the opened cage, sending an army of mice scampering across the floor.

"Radical rodents!" I groan. "Mum's gonna have a fit!"

Mum never wanted us to get pet mice in the first place. She reckoned three guinea pigs, two cats and a tankload of guppies were enough pets for any family *'specially* one as big as ours. But in the end, Billy and I wore her down. (Mind you, if I'd known then how fast a family of mice can multiply, I'd have kept my big mouth shut!)

Don't get me wrong, I like mice. I even like big families (I have to coming from ours). Trouble is, with me and my brother packed together in one titchy bedroom, two rodent cages plus a kitty litter tray not only stink to high heaven, but they take up precious space. (And when you're big, like me, you need *space*.)

So that's where our brilliant Saturday Club comes in...

There's masses of space there. It used to be an old café when me and the gang (Izzie, Jen and Brains) found it last term and we had a big fight to turn it into a clubhouse, organizing a protest march and everything. But in the end we got so much support that the council, led by the infamous Councillor Graham, had to give way (ha, ha!).

Now not only the gang, but a whole load more kids meet there every Saturday and it's the best thing ever to hit Big Rock. Let's face it, us big kids need a place where we can get away from annoying little brothers and escaped mice!

"Wee wee wee." One of those

mice is now squeaking and running up the ladder on to my bunk-bed. "Wee wee wee..." Billy makes a lunge as it scurries across my Superman duvet. "Wee-wee weeee..."

"Get him off!"

Too late. Before you can say "wee-wee" there's a dark yellow stain creeping right across Superman's pants.

"Jibbering jellybabies!" I shout. "Superman's wet the bed!" and we burst out laughing.

But Mum, coming in to see what the noise is all about, is not so amused. She can't see the funny side of chasing mice up curtains and behind radiators especially when one of them gets lost behind Billy's Practical Jokes Kit, and Billy and me start to muck about with his rude-noise cushion.

"Can't wait to try this out in assembly on April Fool's Day," I say and Billy laughs as I let out a huge raspberry noise from the cushion.

"You'd better not!" Mum says crisply. "Now get these wretched creatures back in their cages!" (She's in a real mood now.)

Mind you, by the time we've got all the little beasts safely locked up, Mum's not the only one in a mood. I'm late for Saturday Club, the baby's bawling, Lulu's spilt her juice and Billy has set up his usual Saturday whine of 'take me to the Saturday Club, take me to the Saturday Club...'

"Take you to my club, Little Bro?" I say putting on my sunglasses and preparing for a quick exit. *"Over my dead body."*

But Mum's ready to risk my threat.

She says dead body or not, I have to take my little brother to the club.

"There's no way I can take Billy and Lulu *and* the baby trekking round the shops," she sighs. "If there was a supermarket over this side of town it'd be different but..."

"Aaaalright, Mum," I say quickly, "I'll take *Lulu* off your hands, then." And before Billy has time to squawk 'Hey, what about me?', I pick up my little sister and make my escape.

You might ask why I'd rather take a baby sister than a little brother to my club, but then you've never met Billy and his Practical Jokes Kit. The truth is, even if Billy wasn't the sneakiest practical joker in the universe, I'd always rather take Lulu because *she* doesn't try to get into my things. And at three years old, she's also easier to boss around.

Besides, there's a special reason why I don't mind taking Lulu today...

Lulu has a buggy. (Just what I need to carry the wood for making ramps!) Today we're going to make wooden ramps for our bike rally, and since my dad's a carpenter I'm Chief Wood Bringer.

That's what Izzie told me yesterday, anyway. She said Brains had to work out the measurements, Jen had to bring the tools and I had to bring wood.

Izzie, Isabel Fossey that is, just loves to organize. Brains calls her Bossy Fossey, because of it (which Izzie hates) but I don't mind her telling us what to do. You only have to look at the way Izzie organized our famous Saturday Club Protest to know she's good at getting things done.

The great thing about our gang is that each of us is good at something. Take Brains, the guy with a head full of more gruesome facts than the Chamber of Horrors. He's great at inventing things. That (plus his brilliant brain) is the reason why we call him Brains. The name Brian Staines just didn't seem to fit the guy who invented the famous Lazy Person's Automatic Nose-picker.

Not everyone appreciates Brains' inventions though. Izzie reckons a mechanical finger picking your nose is not half as much fun as the real thing and Jenna (she's the freckly one with the red hair) says the Nose-picker is not only the most disgusting thing she's ever seen but a waste of a good battery.

Jenna is a bit of a princess about clothes and dirt and all that, but she's brilliant at acting. She's known as Jen Dean Drama Queen because she sometimes (like *all* the time) goes over the top. She's the one in our gang famous for falling in love as often as she falls down (which is all the time with our accident-prone Drama Queen).

As for me, I'm tall, cool and I'm tough – *and they call me Big Max.* (Hey, that sounds like a song!) I'm really into music. I love making up raps and stuff which Mum says is just like her dad. I've never met my drummer grandpa because he lives in Jamaica but Mum says his music is really something. He should hear ours in rough tough Big Rock!

Big Rock may be rough and tough but our gang thinks it's great. And as the founder members of the Saturday Club we are keen to spread the word. Trouble is, we've spread the word so much that the club's already bursting at the seams!

You have to be in the top juniors to join the Saturday Club (*sorry* Billy, you're too young!) and so far there are about thirty members. Kala Patak will be a member just as soon as her dad gives in, then there's Baz Hay, who joined us last year when we had our famous battle with the Bench Boys. Baz is the tall, skinny guy with a lop-sided grin and hair like a haystack. I wasn't sure of him at first – thought he was a bit of a thief – but now I've decided he's all right. He never complains about having no mum or dad around or having to live with his gran. And he's a dead cool artist, the one who designed our Saturday Club sign with the strong man chiselling out the words from a giant rock. That's the sign I see through the trees as Lulu and I reach the top of the hill...

"Yay, Saturday Club!"

I throw myself across the loaded buggy and go whizzing and bumping down the hill towards the old kiddies' playground, with Lulu running after me.

CRASH!

Unfortunately I also crash-land into some official-looking man with a strange sort of camera on a tripod.

"What the blazes are you playing at?" the angry man hollers. "You've just *ruined* a whole morning's work! We'll have to do those measurements all over again!" He bends over to pick up his camera thing, and I get a wonderful view of his big bottom with a Betta Industries plc badge on

the back pocket...
    Betta Industries? Measurements?
    What's he on about?

SATURDAY CLUB

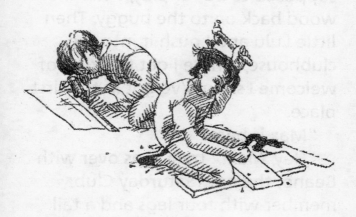

I want to yell back, 'What are *you* playing at! This is a kid's playground and you're no kid!' but I don't. On the other side of the empty sandpit is the Betta Industries' partner and that makes two against one.

So rubbing my bruised behind and muttering under my breath about how playgrounds are supposed to be for play, I pile the wood back on to the buggy. Then little Lulu and I push it into the clubhouse, where I get the kind of welcome I should've got in the first place.

"Max is here!"

"Hey, Max!" Izzie runs over with Beano, the only Saturday Club member with four legs and a tail. They say dogs are like their owners and in Izzie's case it's true. Both are full of energy and both have long hair which hangs in their eyes (though in Izzie's case, the eyes are green, not brown).

"Woof, woof!" goes Beano,

wagging his scruffy tail.

"Max has brought the wood for the ramps!"

"Excellent!"

Everyone crowds round the buggy, examining the pile and shouting to be heard over the racket.

As usual, the clubhouse is really jumping. Megan, Jude and Den are working on a dance routine to music pounding out of the ghetto blaster, there's a noisy game of cards going on and in the corner a group of girls are killing themselves laughing over a pile of comics.

It's your typical Saturday Club morning.

"Hiya!" Roz, our cheerful club leader, is rolling out a massive lump of clay on the art table. You can't miss Roz, she's always so colourful.

Today she's wearing a multi-coloured shirt and her mass of plaits is tied back in a yellow scarf. "Want to make something in clay, Lulu?" she calls out.

Lulu nods her little head so hard, the bobbles on her head shake. "Yeth pleathe!"

As she runs over to the art table, I breathe a sigh of relief and give Roz the thumbs up.

Finally I can do my own thing!

"Come and look at these plans for the bike ramps." Brains has spread out a large sheet of paper on the floor. "I've calculated exactly what we need. First we have to make equal triangles for the sides. Then we make the support struts…" The mathematical genius has worked out the dimensions of the ramps to the last millimetre.

"These look great, Brains!"

"Yeah," Baz gives his lop-sided grin. "Brilliant!"

"Your professor-mind does come in useful sometimes." (Izzie can never resist teasing Brains and the two of them are forever getting into fights.)

Brains makes a face at Izzie then goes into one of his long, detailed explanations about making "accurate measurements". It goes on for so long Izzie uses the time to hand out the markers while Jen sets us up with tools and I sort out the wood. The planks are so big we have to take everything outside in the end so we can spread out.

Rob and Sue, who came top of their classes in CDT, are joining the gang on this project to make sure we do a proper job. Rob used to be a member of our rival gang, the Bench Boys, but he's definitely one of us now. As for Sue, she's brilliant with a hammer and nails. As Jen says, we need experts like them. (What Jen doesn't mention is that we need people like Rob so she can have one of her crushes on them!)

After a bit of discussion, we all get cracking, measuring and marking up the wood for our own ramps (while Beano finds himself a tasty bit to gnaw on). We're making various sizes of ramps and each one has four main pieces with smaller bits for support. It takes for ever with Brains breathing down our necks but even though Izzie thinks wobbly ramps might be more fun, Brains is right to make sure we do it properly. We don't want our bike rally to be a total disaster like the time we made the assault course and everything fell apart after one go!

Soon we've got a whole pile of wood measured out, ready for cutting up. Mind you, it's hungry work. (If I don't eat something soon I might try gnawing on a bit of wood like Beano...)

"I'm starving! Who's on snack duty today?"

"Dunno, but I smell toast," says Izzie, wiping her hands on her jeans. "Come on!"

The toaster and kettle are the best donations the club was ever given and we like to make the most of them. At first we got into loads of arguments about people hogging the toaster, but then Izzie, the great organizer, worked out a rota system. Now everyone takes it in turn to bring the snack and make the toast.

Jeff Higgins and Den Goodman are doing their bit today, handing out buttered toast and hot chocolate. There's a lot of jostling and pushing in and Jeff shouts, "Cool it!" about fifty times, but eventually everybody gets a share.

It's not like school in our club, with lots of rules. Here, we just tell each other off if there's a problem. It usually works, though some people can get a bit too bossy (Izzie Fossey, not to mention any names!).

The tradition at snack time is that everyone finds somewhere to sit so we can talk about what we're doing for the day. You can always find a space on the rug or the arm of a chair.

"We have to check out the park for the best place for the rally," says

Izzie, leaning against the sagging sofa and munching on buttered toast. "Beano, SIT!" She pushes away Beano who's drooling as usual.

"How about round by the paddling pool?" says Jen, unaware that Beano's sneaked up behind the sofa and wolfed down her last piece of toast. "We could ride down the slopes and... hey, what happened to my... BEANO!"

It's while everyone's laughing at Jen's outraged expression that I remember why the paddling pool might not work. "It'll be great to set up our rally at the playground," I agree *"if* it hasn't been taken over!"

"Taken over? Who by? The Bench Boys?"

I shake my head. The Bench Boys fought us last year, when we got the clubhouse, but they're the least of our problems now. With a bitter sigh, I drop the bombshell about the Betta Industries men working in the kiddies' playground. "They aren't from the council, so what are they doing?"

"Maybe they're building a new playground," says Sue hopefully.

"Dream on. There's never enough money for what *we* want."

"Perhaps they're photographers," suggests Jen. "Taking pictures to show how Big Rock Park has gone downhill."

I shake my head. "It wasn't that kind of camera. They were doing some kind of measuring with it."

"We must find out what they're up to," says Izzie, ever ready to fight for our rights.

"Yeah."

We decide to check the Betta men out while Brains, Rob and Sue work on the ramps. Since there are only two saws, it's a good time for some detective work (and our gang is always ready for that).

But just as we're leaving, Lulu runs up and puts a hand sticky with clay into mine. "I want to dig in the thand," she says afraid as always of missing out on anything.

I sigh. "There isn't any sand in the sandpit, Lulu. You stay here."

Lulu's chin starts to wobble.

"I w-want to come."

"Aaalright... But you'd better not get in the way." (I'm a complete pushover when it comes to Lulu and her chin-wobbling routine, and she knows it.)

Over at the kiddies' playground, the Betta Industries man and his tripod have hardly moved a millimetre. He's still looking through his special camera thing at his partner who's holding up a kind of giant measuring stick.

What are they up to?

We reckon I'm not the best person to find out, so Jen (who's the expert at charming grown-ups) goes over to the men, all smiles.

But when she comes back, Jen's face has turned white as rice pudding and her freckles are all blotchy. "They... they're surveyors," she says in a shaky voice. "People who measure up land for building."

"Building!?"

"They can't build here!"

"But they are!" Jen wrings her hands dramatically. "They wouldn't tell me what they're building, but they said it's got nothing at all to do with a kids' playground."

"No...oo..."

"Look at them!" I hiss. "They're measuring up the paddling pool... the sandpit, *even our swings!*"

"They can't pull our swings down!"

"Oh, can't they! Just watch them!" Poor Jen is struggling to hold back her tears.

But Lulu doesn't even try. She looks at the empty sandpit and howls.

"I want to play in the thand! I want to play in the thand!"

•3•

INVASION

Our gang is on the track of a
mystery.

We're going to find out what's
happening to our park and stop it.

35

(The Saturday Club gang is ace at solving mysteries, especially ones that involve fighting for our rights!) So we're going to storm the council offices, beat them into submission, demand they show us the Betta Industries plans....

But first we have to take Lulu back to the club.

This work is not for babies.

And until we find out more, it's not for other club members either. Mysteries like this are best solved in secret.

So secret we can't explain to Brains why we're dragging him away from his ramp-building until we're almost at the council offices. But when we do, he gets so fired up, his glasses fog over with the heat. "The park is public property!" he splutters. "Council regulations give us the right to see their plans."

Izzie grins. "Good thing Brains is such a know-all."

"Yeah, but I'm *bigger,*" I joke and everybody laughs.

The Saturday Club Gang is back in action!

Trouble is, when we reach the council offices, all our plans fall flat because the stupid council offices are closed on Saturdays.

For a minute we're stumped. Then I get the brilliant idea of looking through the windows of the private meeting rooms round the back so we race round there, with Beano bounding ahead barking excitedly (he loves adventure as much as we do).

The back of the building is surrounded by a high wall and locked gate but that is no problem to our gang.

"Come on!"

Beanpole Izzie and me are first to climb the wall (Baz is tall like us, but he hasn't had so much practice climbing). And we're just about to haul the others up after us when we see something which stops us in our tracks...

"Ssshhh..."

An army of uniformed men are unloading containers from lorries – plastic body-sized containers, hundreds of them. As one lorry backs up another pulls in, packed full with the things.

Whatever's inside them?

And why are they making a delivery on *Saturday*, the very day the council offices are closed? There's something creepy about the way the men move in deadly earnest.

Silently, like robots, they wheel the containers down the ramps and line them up, one-by-one with machine-like precision.

It reminds me of a film I saw where aliens unloaded these giant pod things which grew into human doubles while the people were sleeping (so the aliens could get rid of the humans and put alien clones in their place).

What if there are pods inside those containers!

Two uniformed guards with clipboards are checking off the deliveries. Izzie and I strain to hear what they are saying.

"We'll make the change-over this week," says the first.

"Won't be easy," says the other. "People will squawk."

"They'll soon get used to it."

"What about the grannies?"

"No problem. *You just tip 'em up and push 'em.*"

Izzie and I look at one another, horrified. Are these robots planning to carry off the innocent grannies of Big Rock? In silent agreement, we jump back down to the others.

"What's going on?" Jen whispers.

"Gang, you're not going to like this..."

"Tell us!"

"*Big Rock is being invaded.*"

4

A STRANGE GRAVEYARD

"The aliens have landed!" Izzie
announces as dramatically as the
Drama Queen herself.

Jen gasps but Baz only raises an

eyebrow. *"You're joking!"*

"See for yourself," I drop my voice to a mysterious whisper. "It's like *Invasion of The Alien Body Snatchers* over there."

Brains' glasses nearly pop off his nose. "According to my calculations that wasn't supposed to happen until the next century..."

"Ssshhh..." Already I can hear the lorries revving up to go (finished with their dirty work).

We wait until the last one has pulled out. Then Baz and I are the first over the wall. "Look!" I say, pointing to the rows of body-sized containers. "Your granny'd better watch out, because we heard them planning to..."

But before I can finish my warning, Baz interrupts me with a shout of laughter. "They're wheelie bins!" he laughs. "Nothing but wheelie bins!"

"Wheelie bins?"

"For your rubbish. Everybody had them where I used to live." Baz is practically wetting himself.

"What's so funny?" I give him a shove. "Eh? Eh? Okay, so they're wheelie bins... The point is what's *inside them?"* And just to prove I'm no wimp, I run straight over to one of the bins and fling open the lid – only to find the stupid thing's empty!

Phew!

Mind you, there is something stuck inside the lid of the wheelie bin that's more suspicious than a whole barrel of alien pods... It's a label that reads Betta Industries plc.

The plot thickens.

I'm just trying to figure this out,

when there's a scream from Jen who's climbed the wall further along and lost her footing. "Aaaaghhh!" yells our accident-prone drama queen as she disappears into the side yard with a crash!

"Stay there, Jen! I'm coming!" I dash over to the side, scale the wall and leap down, making an even bigger crash as I land on a huge mountain of empty dustbins on the other side.

CRASH!

"Help!" a little voice comes from under a pile of rusty bins. "Help!"

I clamber over the mountain of bins to Jen as with even more clattering and banging, the others jump down to join us.

"Wow!"

"What's this?"

"It's a dustbin graveyard!"

The gang crashes about on the pile, laughing and making jokes about alien smells. (Beano thinks he's died and gone to heaven, because even though the rusty, metal bins haven't been used in ages the smell of old rubbish still clings to them.)

I'm just about to tell the gang about the Betta Industries label, when Baz, who hasn't stopped killing himself laughing yet, says, "Max thought *aliens* had left a load of wheelie bins!"

"I only said the men *looked* like aliens!"

Baz snorts.

"*Don't Baz,*" pleads Izzie. "You know Max can't stand being laughed at."

She's right.

I'd rather be boiled in oil, and

eaten by ants than be laughed at.
I pick up two big lids and bash them
together angrily. "If you'd seen
what we saw you wouldn't laugh!"
I shout.

"Stop it!" Jen begs. "Someone
will hear you."

"See if I care!" I retort bashing
away.

"Don't worry, Jen," chuckles Baz.
"Enemy aliens haven't taken over
Big Rock yet."

"Yeah, and we won't let them!" I
snarl, though I'm thinking of the
real enemy – Betta Industries.

"Too right!" Izzie picks up a stick.
"The aliens have gone!" she shouts,
banging in time with the clashes of
my lids. *"The aliens have gone!"*

Suddenly the whole gang starts
mucking about with the dustbins,
using the lids as cymbals and

bashing the bins like drums, cheering and shouting, "The aliens have gone! The aliens have gone!"

The rhythms are so great, they drum all the anger out of me. And moving my body in time with the beat, I get going with one of my super-dooper raps:

> *"Bang that drum!*
> *Listen to my song!*
> *Let's have fun...*
> *The aliens have gone!"*

Everyone joins in as we play our own steel band.

It's terrific.

Aliens or not, one thing's for sure – our gang knows how to have fun!

What they don't know yet is that Betta Industries are more powerful than we first suspected. And, as I

beat my drum and shout out my
rap, the thought runs through me
over and over again...

What can we do to stop them?

5

THE EASTER BUNNY

I'm thinking about this, still rapping away when I get the kind of brainwave that *should* send me to the top of the class.

"Hey! These dustbins would be great to manoeuvre round in our bike rally," I say. "And a spectacular rally like that would show everyone who's boss of the park..."

"The Saturday Club!"

"Exactly."

Everyone thinks my idea is great. We all agree that the more the Saturday Club holds events in Big Rock Park, the more chance we have of keeping it the way we want it.

"If we can get people on our side we can't lose," says Izzie. "Look at our protest last year."

"You said it."

Everybody starts offering ideas on using the bins then. Brains reckons if we weight them on their sides we could put bolts through them and screw planks on to them. That way we could ride our bikes down the slopes. We could even make bridges and balance our bikes across them.

"How about drumming the bins while the rally's going on?" suggests Izzie. "Like they did in medieval jousting contests."

"Cool!" I lunge at Baz and the two of us start into our own jousting match using the dustbin lids as shields.

"Ooof! Ooof!"

"Aaaggghhh..."

"Stop it, you two!" says Izzie. "Save your energy to fight for our park."

She's right, I suppose.

Reluctantly Baz and I leave off fighting and everyone gets down to choosing their own bin. (Though naturally we can't convince Jen that the germs on these bins expired centuries ago and she makes a big fuss about picking the cleanest ones.)

Then Baz and Izzie climb over the wall and we roll the bins over the top to them. (It makes a brilliant racket.)

We troop through Big Rock Park, dragging and banging the lids against the dustbins as we go.

Our gang won't be beaten down.

Back at the clubhouse, everyone is as pleased as punch with our find, especially when we tell them the bins have just been dumped and there are loads more.

"I could use some of them for storing things," says Roz, who's clearing away the clay. "You'll have to go back and get some more."

"We will."

"Let's talk about it over lunch."

"Okay."

Suddenly everyone is bustling about cleaning the tables and getting out food.

Lunch-time is brilliant at the club, but it wasn't always so good. Everyone used to bring their own packed lunches and since there was always someone who forgot, there was never enough to go round. Then Izzie hit on the clever idea of each person bringing as much as they can of only one thing. That way we pool the lot and share it out. (It's much better.) Today there are chicken drumsticks, crisps, apples and a huge mountain of sandwiches.

Delicious.

After that lot we check out the ramps that Sue and Rob have finished. They're dead good. Professional joints and everything.

"They're great, Rob," says Jen, dimpling and flashing her smile at him.

"Yeah great, Sue," I say determined to give Sue a share of the praise. "My dad couldn't have done better and he's a carpenter."

"Thanks."

It's fun making things out of wood. And now that there's a special reason for our bike rally to be a success, we all work doubly hard. For a while I'm so occupied sawing and sanding wood that I almost forget about Betta Industries and Big Rock Park being taken over.

It's only when I'm sawing through my biggest plank of wood that my mind starts going over everything that's happened.

The Betta Industries surveyors, the fact that the wheelie bin delivery was made in secret and the label in the bin... these three things are linked into some kind of master plan.

If only I knew what that plan was.

Zizz zizz goes my saw and with each stroke, the word Betta buzzes through my head... Betta... Betta... Betta.

Usually I'd try to thrash out a problem like this with the gang, but I'm not going to give anyone another reason to laugh at me today, so the word Betta niggles me all afternoon.

And the *weird thing is, when I get home from club, the word hits me all over again!*

Mum's cooking egg and chips for tea. Nothing strange about that. The kitchen is the usual warm, steamy fug with Billy teasing Lulu and the baby banging his spoon like he always does. Nothing strange about that either. What *is* unusual is the egg carton with the Bettafoods logo, part of the Betta Industries group. Mum never goes right over the other side of town to shop at Bettafoods...

"Where did you get the eggs, Mum?" I ask, helping myself to a mound of chips.

Mum turns round, surprised to find me suddenly interested in food shopping. "The Bettafoods supermarket chain were giving out free cartons of eggs in the market place," she says. "As a promotion for Easter."

A promotion for Easter... *oh sure! If that's what this is about, I'm the Easter bunny!*

I'm so deep in thought about this

that I don't notice Billy's swapped
my fried egg for a rubber one until I
bite into it. (He's paying me back for
not letting him come to the club
this morning.)

Very funny.

Well it's lucky for him I don't have
time to get into a fight over it, or
he'd be mincemeat. But right now
I've got a more important battle to
fight than one with my pesky little
brother...

*And that's the battle with Betta
Industries.*

•6•

BIG ROCK TIMES

Betta Industries have got to be stopped.

First they measure up our park, then they make a secret delivery and now they're bribing people with free gifts.

What will be next?

Whatever it is, I have to tell the gang my suspicions, before they try anything else. Things are too serious now for me to waste time worrying about being laughed at.

I have to be a man about it.

So I get on the phone and tell the gang to ride over to the park and meet me at the place where we always used to hang out – the swings.

And when they get there it feels so like old times, I wonder why I'm worried about my friends laughing at me. The point is, even though we've come a long way since we only had four swings, a broken duck and a horse bent off its rocker, we've still got a fight on our hands... *And that's the most important thing.*

Taking a deep breath, I tell the gang all about it: the label, my suspicions about the secret delivery and the free eggs. "And the label I found in the wheelie bin was the *same label* that was on the surveyor's pocket," I say finally. "Now that can't be coincidence."

"Chances are about a million to one," Brains says (and he should know).

"This park is ours," Jen waves her arms about as if she's making a speech onstage. "How can we get those surveyors to tell us what they're planning to build? *How?*"

"Why don't we tie them up and tickle them to death with my Automatic Nose-picker?" says Brains and we crack up laughing.

But Jen only gives one of her big, melodramatic sighs. "Couldn't we just report Betta Industries to the police?" she says tragically.

"Jumping jellybeans! That's it!" I clap my hand to my head. "Jen, you're brilliant!"

"Huh?"

"We won't report them. We'll get a *reporter* to help us!" Steve Marker, our friendly reporter, works at the *Big Rock Times* Newspaper offices. "Steve *must* know something."

"Good thinking, Big Max!" says Baz, his blue eyes crinkling into a lop-sided smile. "That's a brilliant plan."

"Come on," I say, glad to find Baz doesn't think I'm such an idiot after all. "We've no time to lose!"

We jump back on our bikes and

ride over to the *Big Rock Times* offices. Fast.

And we're in luck. Even though it's gone seven, and it's a Saturday, Steve is still there typing away at his computer. (You have to work all hours on a newspaper.)

"Hmmm... a building in the park?" says Steve when we tell him about the surveyors. "That would have to be approved by the City Planners."

He explains that in Big Rock any building proposal must be published in the paper at least six months before surveying begins. "I remember reporting something about selling off public land when I was doing my piece about Big Rock Park last year."

"Then we're too late!" Jen cries, clutching her heart. "Oh Steve, what shall we do? *What shall we do?"*

Steve takes off his famous glasses (the ones that are taped together with elastoplast) and smiles at Jen.

"Well… the six months is only just up. We could look through the back-dated papers and find out when the council is meeting."

"Great!"

"Hang on while I open up the file…" says Steve inserting a disc labelled 'Big Rock Park' into his computer and clicking open a file on the screen. "Here we are… I made a report about land sale proposals in November last year. Let's take a look at the newspaper for that time. We keep a copy here of every one we've ever printed."

"Great!"

Excitedly, we follow Steve into the place he calls 'The Archives' which is a kind of huge warehouse stacked to the top with old papers. It's like the secret files of MI5.

We're really on the trail of Betta Industries now...

Steve goes down the rows until he finds the date he's looking for. "Here it is..." he turns the pages to a small item on the next to last page. "'Council Proposal to Sell off Public Land for Development. Meeting Scheduled 1 April, 8.30 p.m.'"

"April Fools! That's Monday!"

Perfect day for them!

Well, they're not going to trick us into losing our club. If the council is going to meet about our park, the gang will be there. Then we'll see who are the biggest April Fools in Big Rock.

April Fools reminds me of another trickster... my sneaky little brother.

Normally I wouldn't bother about getting even while I'm busy with important work like this. But what keeps niggling me is that Billy won't stop at a rubber egg now. Before you know it, there'll be itching powder in my pants, fake ink blots on my homework and plastic dog poo in my bath. We'll get into a huge punch up and since it won't be me who'll get hurt, *I'll* be the one who ends up being grounded.

I can't risk that.

I have to be free to stop Betta Industries from taking over our park. So before we leave the archives, I ask Steve if I can borrow a copy of last year's newspaper for Monday 31 March.

I have a plan that will stop Billy in his tracks.

And on Monday morning I'm ready with the back-dated paper when Billy comes into the kitchen. "April Fool!" he sings out, waggling a stupid fake spider in my face.

"It's not April Fool's Day yet," I say pointing to the date on my old newspaper. "It's the 31st of March."

"Huh....?"

"You'll have to wait a whole year to play your tricks at school, Little Bro. The Easter holidays start tomorrow."

The look on Billy's face tells me my plan has worked.

At last I can stop worrying about getting into a punch up, and concentrate on Betta Industries. What's more, a victory over my sneaky little brother is just what I need to give me confidence for what I must do today.

Because the trick our gang is about to play is far more dangerous than altering any date.

STAKE OUT

It's dark.

The trees are blotting out the sky and all you can see is the looming dark shape of the council building.

Dead creepy.

"I'm scared," Jen whimpers.

"Put on your torch."

Quick and silent as thieves, we climb over the back wall of the council building. We're inside the backyard now, Izzie, Brains, Jen, Baz, Beano and me plus about six hundred wheelie bins. It's weird.

Suddenly a light goes on and we duck down.

From behind the bins we see that one of the rooms is lit up like a Christmas tree. This must be a special meeting room because it's not grey like the other council offices but newly decorated with fancy wallpaper and chandeliers. The new carpet looks like velvet. In the middle of the room are two long polished tables pushed together and at the far end is a raised platform with another long table. Behind it is a big metal easel.

We watch in silence as the council members file in and take their places at the table.

The meeting begins.

Trouble is, we can't tell what the meeting's about outside here. Inside that fancy room the councillors are sure to be discussing our future, but we can't hear a thing.

Beside me Beano, feeling the tension, whines softly.

The meeting goes on and on and everyone is starting to look as bored as I feel. But just as I'm beginning to wonder why we bothered to come, Beano stiffens and gives a low growl of recognition.

He's seen our old enemy, Councillor Graham.

Councillor Graham, the man who

tried to stop us having a Saturday Club (the man Izzie nicknamed 'Hairy Nose' because of his amazingly long nasal hairs), steps up on to the raised platform and clips a huge plan on to the easel.

Suddenly the room is electric.

The council members have woken up at the sight of Hairy Nose's plan because they are suddenly talking heatedly, banging the table and shaking their heads.

Hairy Nose points to the plan over and over again, hits it, waves his arms about and goes red in the face.

The councillors shout.

Hairy Nose shouts back.

It's bedlam in there.

Then, before you know it, things start to calm down. Two of the councillors seem to be reconsidering and they look like they're trying to convince the others. Hairy Nose must be winning because they're starting to nod in agreement.

What's he getting them to agree to?

I strain to see what's written on Hairy Nose's plan, but it's not until he steps to one side that I'm able to read what's written across the top— 'BETTAFOODS SUPERMARKET, BIG ROCK PARK'.

So that's their game!

Hairy Nose is in league with Betta Industries. He's plotting with them to tear down the kids' playground and build a rotten supermarket!

Next thing you know it will be our clubhouse.

As the full impact of this hits me, Izzie squeezes my arm hard, and Jen groans faintly. But before I have a chance to speak, Beano gives a bloodcurdling growl and a dark shape looms up at the window, blocking out the light.

The game's up!

Hairy Nose's face contorts with rage as he sees us crouched down amongst the bushes. He raps on the window. "WHAT ARE YOU KIDS DOING HERE?"

What are we doing? We're running, that's what, we're doing!

Running for our lives!

Over the wall we go, round to the front of the building and down the street, and we don't stop running till we get home.

What a night!

But it's not over yet.

Back home, I'm just about to climb into my bunk bed when I notice something glistening in the moonlight...

It's a retractable dagger, stained with fake blood, and it has skewered a page from the back-dated newspaper I tricked Billy with on to my pillow. I switch on my torch, so I can look at it without waking Billy and all the other little rodents.

Scrawled across the page is a message written in blood (actually red felt pen).

"You'll be sorry..." the message says.

Huh.

So Billy thinks he can scare me with threats like that!

Little does he know, to someone like me (who risks his neck fighting the mighty forces of Betta Industries and Hairy Nose Graham) a poison pen letter stuck to a toy dagger is about as scary as a pop-up picture book of monsters!

But, tearing off the newspaper I get a surprise that *does* make me gasp. There on the page is a picture of our old enemy Hairy Nose Graham with a line-up of smiling men (and two of the men were the ones who changed their minds at tonights' council meeting).

The caption under the photograph reads:

"Main Shareholders at Betta Industries plc Annual Meeting... Councillor Robert Graham, main shareholder, shown here with other major shareholders, is all smiles. 'We believe the value of these shares is sure to go up,' says Councillor Graham."

You'll make sure of it, you mean!
So that's why you want to get
Betta Industries to buy our land.
No wonder those two other council
members changed their minds too.

"Well, well, Councillor Graham..."
I whisper to myself, reading again
Billy's message in blood. "I think
you are going to be the one who's
sorry..."

·8·

SHOCK TACTICS

It's time to spill the beans.

The Betta Industries takeover. The councils' involvement and Hairy Nose's plan to have them build a supermarket in Big Rock Park. We've got to let Roz in on it.

Luckily our club is open for the Easter holidays, so it gives us a chance to tell her before the other members arrive.

And when we do she's furious.

"This is outrageous!" she fumes and her dark face, usually so happy, is a picture of anger. "We've got to stop them!"

"But how?"

"What about a protest, like we held for the club?" suggests Izzie.

Roz shakes her head. "Somehow we have to show people that destroying the Kids' Park will be a real loss to the community... Which won't be easy since they've let the place get so run-down. I suspect Councillor Graham has been planning this for a long time.

Probably the reason he didn't want the club in the first place." (Roz may be a teenager, but she knows a thing or two.)

"When I was little I always played in the playground," Izzie says sadly. "It was really nice."

"Now there's nowhere for little kids to play," I say remembering Lulu's cry of, *"I want to play in the thand!"* We big kids have got the club (even if it is under threat), but the little ones have got nothing.

We're so deep in discussion about all this that we hardly notice the other club members filtering in. One by one they gather round the sofa and listen to our story and it's not long before the whole Saturday Club knows.

Big Rock Park is in danger.

"I think we should sack the

councillors," Megan Carter says.

"Boil them in oil!" suggests bloodthirsty Kirsty.

Everyone starts speaking at once then. We all want to find a way to save our park, but suggestions like letting off stink bombs in the council chambers, or turning the council car-park into a playground are not very helpful. What we really need to fight the enemy is a huge sum of cash.

If we had money we could improve the playground. If we had money we could fight the council.

It gets me so frustrated, I jump up on to the sofa like some rebel leader making a speech. "So we don't have money!" I shout. "Then why don't we make some!"

"How can *we* make money?" says Jack Wilson, one of the kids who left the Bench Boys to join our club. "My dad can't make any."

Luckily I don't have to answer this question, because the other members are so fired up they're falling over themselves to give out their money-making ideas. There are suggestions like applying to the lottery fund, writing to the Queen or getting a millionaire to sponsor us (one kid even suggests robbing a bank!). Trouble is, none of these ideas seems very likely.

Then Izzie comes up with the brilliant idea of a fundraiser. A huge money-making sort of fête in the park with stalls and sponsored events starting with the Bike Rally.

"If we hold a fundraiser we can make money *and* get public support to stop the supermarket at the same time!" she says excitedly.

Suddenly it's as if a dam has burst. Everyone makes so many suggestions, Brains is forced to write them down in the "Gruesome Facts" notebook he carries with him.

And this is what we come up with:

Fundraiser to Save the Playground
1. *Stalls (crafts, pottery and handmade stuff)*
2. *Bike Rally (get sponsors)*
3. *Face-painting*
4. *Raffle*
5. *Auction of promises*
6. *Charge to paint paddling pool*
7. *Toddler parade round playground*
8. *Demonstration of inventions (including Automatic Nose-picker)*
9. *Tombola*
10. *Tug of War*
11. *Coconut-shy*
12. *Hoopla*

It's brilliant.

Everyone volunteers to do different things on the list and the club leaps into immediate action.

Roz sets up a large group at the craft table and the face-painting team go off to practise their designs. Den, Megan and Jude work on taping music from the ghetto-blaster and the Baker twins make a list of requests for donations (top of the list being coconuts from the greengrocers).

Another group starts organizing the Tombola collection and a bunch of girls gets busy mixing paints for printing wrapping paper and cards. While this is going on, Roz takes down "promises" to auction at the fundraiser (promises to do babysitting, mow the lawn or do the shopping).

As for our gang...
It's time for us to try out our Bike Rally.

ACCUSED

*"We got the ramps,
We got the bins!
We are the champs,
We're gonna win!"*

We're rapping in rhythm with the noise the bins make as we roll them across to the playground, bump, bump bump.

"Right," says Izzie. "Let's put two bins over by the swings and a ramp by the sandpit..."

"No, we have to put the ramp for the paddling pool there," says Brains who feels he owns this rally.

"Don't be daft! We need to do the weaving in and out of bins there!"

"Look, Bossy Fossey!" Brains shouts. "I designed the ramps. *And I say where the ramps go!*"

"All right, all right... don't go on a *rampage* about it!" I joke and everyone laughs. "Anyway, who was it said we need to save our fight for the real enemy?"

Izzie sighs. "I know, I know."

And so we set up the rally without any more arguments.

As soon as we've got the bins and ramps and planks in position we fetch our bikes.

Then Izzie, Baz and I take off fast, whizzing round the bins and shooting up the ramps, doing dead professional wheelies and turns.

It's like a Formula One race!

Through the rows of bins I go, looping round the swings with Izzie in front and Baz behind me. Under the swing pole I race, circling the sandpit, riding up the ramp and down into the pool.

It's ace.

And as I race into the wind, a great whoosh of power shoots through me. With this Bike Rally in our fundraiser, we *will* beat the enemy.

We will, we will, we will...

But back at the clubhouse, all my excitement is squashed. Deflated like a burst balloon...

Because standing there talking to Roz is the enemy himself... Councillor Graham.

His miserable face is all squeezed up with frowns and he's going on and on, moaning in that whiny voice of his about trespassing on council property, spying on private meetings and young trouble-makers who ought to be punished.

Roz looks really upset. "I promise you it won't happen again, Councillor Graham," she says.

"It certainly won't!"

"We didn't mean any harm," says Jen sweetly. "We were only walking our dog."

Old Hairy Nose gives a snort, sending those famous nose hairs of his dancing (and Izzie and I have to stifle our laughter). Then he launches into yet another attack, and this time it's more serious.

This time it's about stealing.

Seems he's found out about the dustbins and he's making a big deal about them being council property. *Stolen* council property, he says. He orders them to be returned. Says they're being recycled.

(Huh! Well we're gonna cycle round them!)

"I shall be writing to the parents of the youngsters concerned," Hairy Nose finishes triumphantly. "We cannot allow a club to continue if its members steal from the council."

"We'll return the bins, Councillor

Graham," says Roz. "We'll pay for..."

"That's not good enough. I shall have to meet with the committee about this," interrupts Hairy Nose. "There will be *repercussions.*" Then he slams out of the door and we can hear him get into his posh car and roar off.

"He's the thief! *He's* the one stealing our park!" I growl punching the sofa. "I'd like to sock him right on his hairy nose!"

"Calm down, Max," says Roz. "This won't help."

Calm down? How can I calm down? Hairy Nose Graham is trying to destroy our club. Our only chance of stopping him is with the fundraiser and now even *that* is in danger without the bins for the Bike Rally.

How can we prove to the people of Big Rock that Councillor Graham is corrupt?

There must be a way...

• 10 •

TRUTH TIME

"Izzie, come with me," I whisper. "We need to do a little research at the *Big Rock Times* offices."

"Gotcha." Izzie grins at me like a

conspirator and without another word clips Beano's lead on to his collar.

But over at the *Big Rock Times* offices, we hit a snag. The receptionist won't let us through. She says we can't see Steve Marker because he's out reporting.

"Create a diversion!" I whisper to Izzie. "We've no time to lose."

"Right." (Not for nothing is Izzie the mistress of an over-friendly Border Collie.) Quick as a flash, Izzie gets Beano to offer his paw in friendship to the receptionist who is so occupied with dodging licks and laughing her head off that she doesn't notice me slip by.

Good old Beano!

All I have to do is look as if I belong in the newspaper offices and make my way over to Steve's desk.

Once behind Steve's computer, I'm safe. But safe or not, my heart is banging against my ribs like a steel drum. (Steve wouldn't mind what I'm about to do, but others would, even though it is in a good cause.)

With shaking fingers, I flip through Steve's box of floppy discs, until I find the one I'm looking for – the one labelled 'Big Rock Park'. Quickly, quietly, I switch on the computer and insert the disc.

There are pages and pages of reporting going back to the day when we first saw Steve taking notes on a park bench. Somewhere amongst these notes must be a clue to why Hairy Nose is so keen to destroy our park.

Then I find it.

A list of council expenses for the last year. Big expenses.

Old Hairy Nose has spent a fortune on redecorating the large meeting room with chandeliers, plush carpets and flocked wallpaper (all purchased from Betta Industries, of course). And that's not all. The bill for the Betta wheelie bins is astronomical. So *that's* why they were delivered in secret. Hairy Nose didn't want to draw attention to his big spending.

No wonder he wants to sell off land to cover his tracks!

The council is in debt and it needs the money!

But the council isn't the only organization to make money out of this deal. I already know from the backdated newspaper that as a major shareholder in the company, the value of Hairy Nose's own shares will go shooting up with a new supermarket. Hairy Nose Graham will be rich enough to buy a whole fleet of those expensive cars he likes to drive.

Everything makes sense now.

"Hello. What are you doing here?" a voice by my elbow makes me jump out of my skin.

"Steve! I was just... I was looking up... You won't believe what I've found..." I trail off at the sight of Steve's frown.

"You'd better explain..."

I gulp and begin. And even though Steve's a friend, it takes all my powers of persuasion to make him see that I couldn't wait for him. He says it's a huge breach of rules to look into his files the way I did. But in the end, even he has to agree the information I've unearthed is so crucial there was no time to lose.

"The budget information didn't seem significant when I made note of it last year. It's your putting it all together that makes it a bombshell," says Steve pushing his glasses back up his nose.

"Exactly."

Hairy Nose's overspending is the missing link in the Betta Industries puzzle.

Mind you, tough as convincing Steve is, my troubles aren't over yet. Because when I get in that night, my dad is waiting for me and he looks madder than a hundred Steve Markers.

"What's this Billy tells me about you taking my wood?" he says in a voice that means business.

So that's what Billy meant by his threat!

"Well, Max?"

"Er..." *If Dad's mad about his wood what will he say when he hears about us taking the bins?*

"I'm waiting."

"Dad, I didn't think you'd mind," I say truthfully. "They were only off-cuts you were throwing out."

"You didn't ask, that's the point."

How can I explain to Dad that when I get enthusiastic about things, I just have to go for it? How sometimes I just don't think...

But I don't have to explain, because Dad is saying it all for me. (Boy, is he ever saying it!)

And when this long and punishing lecture is over, Dad glares at me. "Well, Max, what have you got to say for yourself?"

What have I got to say for myself? A lot, that's what.

So taking a deep breath, I let it all

out. I tell Dad about Betta Industries and Hairy Nose Graham's part in it. I tell him about the Big Rock takeover, about our plans for a fundraiser to improve the playground... And finally I even admit to stealing the bins.

What have I got to lose? I'm already in trouble.

To my amazement Dad doesn't blow his stack this time, he just listens to my long and complicated tale. And when I've finished he nods his head thoughtfully.

"Sounds to me like you need a carpenter," is all he says.

"A carpenter?"

"Yep." Dad grins a grin that splits his face in two. "Sounds like you need a carpenter to build that new playground equipment in Big Rock Park."

DISASTER

It's a toss-up what the gang is more pleased about. My discovery of Hairy Nose's corrupt dealings or Dad's promise to help us build a new playground.

Whichever one it is, the gang thinks I'm the bee's knees (and so they should!).

But the next morning, disaster strikes.

I'm feeling in a really good mood as I cycle over to the club in the sunshine, when suddenly I see something that stops me in my tracks and I'm forced to screech to a halt on my bike.

The playground has been demolished!

The whole thing's been bulldozed. Razed to the ground. The swings have been ripped out, the rocking horse removed and the wobbly duck taken.

Those monsters!

I'm still in shock when Jen and Izzie ride up with Beano bounding alongside them.

"What have they done? Oh, what have they done?" cries Jen and she bursts into tears.

"They've destroyed it..." groans Izzie. "The kiddies' playground..."

I put my arm across Izzie's shoulders. "Don't worry, Iz. They can't get away with this," I say.

But is that really true?

Adults like Hairy Nose seem to go ahead and do just what they want. Misuse public money, destroy public places... and all for their own gain.

Looking around us at the devastation, we all feel pretty lost and hopeless. Even poor Beano is confused, and is anxiously searching the flattened ground for precious, remembered smells.

But we won't be beaten for long.

As the rest of the gang rides up,

each of them reacting to the dreadful sight, we're already trying to work out a plan.

If the adults are going to play dirty, we must fight on their terms.

Feeling my courage rise to this challenge, I spur everyone on with the shout, "Big Rock Park's ours and no one's going to take it over!"

"Yeah!"

"Right on!"

It's time to get tough.

First we'll get Steve to write a piece for the newspaper on Hairy Nose Graham and his involvement with Betta Industries.

Then we'll organize a questionnaire for the little kids of Big Rock to say what they want in the playground. (That'll get the mums and dads going!)

Finally we'll speak to Mr Patak.

Mr Patak, who runs the corner shop, is one adult who will be just as angry as we are at the prospect of a supermarket in the park. He's not going to lose business lying down.

So, full of fighting spirit, we race over to Patak's corner shop.

The Patak family lives in a flat above the shop. And as soon as we tell Mr Patak about the supermarket plans, he does something he's never done before. He closes the shop and takes us up. "This is too important to discuss in front of the customers," he says. "Sit down... make yourselves comfortable."

So we sit on big colourful floor cushions while Mrs Patak brings out a whole pile of freshly made poppadams and dips for us to eat.

"My wife makes good food, eh?" says Mr Patak as we dive in.

"Mmmm," I agree munching on a delicious warm poppadam. "She's the best."

"Patak's corner shop will provide the food for the fundraiser," says Mr Patak and Mrs Patak nods in agreement. "We must make lots of money to build a new playground."

"That's great!"

A stall with Indian food will be a real money-spinner at the fundraiser.

"Can I join the Saturday Club now, Dad?" begs Kala seeing her chance. "Please, Dad. Pleeeease..."

Mr Patak looks at his wife. "What do you say, my dear?"

"I always said it would be a good thing," smiles Mrs Patak.

Mr Patak nods. "It is certainly time for us to work together. All right, you may join, Kala."

I knew we were right to go to Mr Patak!

Kala is thrilled to be a member of the Saturday Club at last.

And in a demonstration of our team spirit we discuss ways to fight the building of a supermarket. At our suggestion, Mr Patak promises to get a pile of posters printed saying, "Support Your Local Shop" so we can put them up all over Big Rock.

Next we suggest the Pataks draw up a petition for customers to sign saying they want to keep the shop going.

Then Kala has the great idea of getting the local radio station to have a phone-in about it. "People are sure to have lots to say!" she says.

"Brilliant, Kala!"

It's like the good old days when we protested for the Saturday Club.

No one is going to beat us.

We're the best club in the world, as Kala soon finds out. A great cheer goes up when she enters the clubhouse.

"Welcome to the Saturday Club," says Roz happily. "I knew you'd get here in the end. We need all the help we can get for the fundraiser too. Now what would you like to do?"

"Everything," smiles Kala looking round happily at the clubhouse, which today looks like a mini-factory. "Just everything..."

Everyone is busy working away and there is already a pile of things to sell. There are kids making clay pots, a group weaving neckties and belts and another making papier mâché jewellery. The nature lovers are planting bulbs and drying petals for pot pourri while Baz's lot are painting pictures.

Baz rushes to get out the huge one he started yesterday, of kids splashing in the paddling pool (filled with water like paddling pools are supposed to be). "It's futuristic," he says. "A vision of how our park could be."

"It *will* happen!" I say, thumping him on the back. "We're going to raise so much money our playground will be the best ever." And feeling more determined than ever, I get down to work with Sue and Rob carving door stops from leftover scraps of wood.

As for Izzie, she organizes the questionnaire on the playground equipment. And, naturally, at snack time club members can't resist getting in on the act. (Playgrounds may be for little kids but there are still some things we big kids like.)

Jude is first with an idea. "How about a huge high-wire to slide down with handles like at my cousins' park?" she suggests.

"Ropes to climb!"

"A place to roller blade."

"With a soft rubber surface so you don't scrape your knees..."

"Yeah and an assault course like in the army," says Simon Bowler.

"Too bad we don't have our dustbins," I say munching on a piece of buttered toast. "We could tunnel through them."

But when I get home that night, tired and pleased with all we've done today, I get an unexpected answer to the whole question of the dustbins.

On the kitchen table is a circular. A circular that's been sent out to every home in Big Rock. It says:

**PLEASE CLEAN OUT OLD BINS
TO EXCHANGE FOR
NEW WHEELIE BINS**

Well, this time I'm not going to get accused of stealing bins! This time I ask my dad if I can have our bin *before* I take it.

And when I do, Dad just grins and says the old bins belong to us, so I'm welcome to ours.

Good.

Wasting no time, I phone up the gang. "Bring your bin from home to club tomorrow," I say. "We'll show Hairy Nose his threats can't hurt us."

•12•

FUNDRAISING

Fundraiser Day.

I wake up early to the sound of Lulu singing a little "digging in the sand" song.

*"Dig dig dig the thand,
I'm digging in the thand..."*

My little sister is marching round
the flat, wearing only a swim-suit
and a sunhat (all ready for the
Toddler Parade). I groan as her baby
voice screeches on to a high note
and Lulu, hearing that groan,
promptly climbs up the ladder to
my bunk-bed and hits me with her
spade!

"Ow!"

"I'm digging in the thand, Max!"
she informs me with a big grin.

"Digging me in the ribs, more
like!" I say rubbing my side. "Watch
what you do with that spade."

*It's definitely time for me to get
up.*

Delicious baking smells are
wafting around the flat now

anyway, so I follow my nose to the kitchen.

Mum is in there piling batches of chocolate chip cookies on to a big tray to sell.

"Mmmmm!" I say. "Can I have one?"

"Not yet," says Mum. "Go and help Dad first."

Dad is already outside sorting out wood to take to the fundraiser. We're going to have a big pile so we can get people to "Buy A Plank For The Playground".

So when we've finished with the sorting, we start to load it up. It's heavy work. (Good thing I've got muscles!) We slave away for nearly an hour and I'm sweating when we've finished.

Back in the kitchen Billy is up now, getting under everyone's feet.

"What can I do?" he says following me about and banging into me as I get my plate of cereal. "Tell me what I can do for the fundraiser."

"Why don't you join the Toddler Parade?" I snarl as I wipe spilt milk from my favourite T-shirt. "That's about your age level." (The truth is, I'm still mad at my dear little bro for getting me into trouble with Dad.)

Billy reddens, points his tongue at me and runs out of the kitchen to the hall.

"Hey, wait! Mum needs you to help her with…"

"You'll be sorry!" he shouts before I have a chance to finish and he slams out of the front door.

What a temper!

But it's not until I get to the downstairs hall, that I find out why

Billy was in such a hurry.

That rotten kid has taken my bike!

My twelve-gear mountain bike with the fluorescent mudguards has gone and all that's left is Billy's stupid bike (the one that used to be mine before I grew out of it) and Lulu's little pink one with the silver fairy bell.

I'm going to spifflicate that kid...

The park is filling up quickly.

The hot sun and the crowds give a wonderful holiday feel to the day. People stroll about, stopping at the stalls to look and to buy. The kids are eager to try the Hoopla stall and the Pin the Tail on the Rocking Horse.

Ahhhh... the tinkle of money falling into the biscuit tins is music to my ears!

Delicious spicy smells waft about as people walk by with their paper plates of Indian food. "Here, have an onion bhajee," Kala smiles and offers me a sample, "before we run out."

"Roll up, roll up for the coconut shy!" The Baker twins are doing a roaring trade.

"Raffle tickets! Buy your raffle tickets here!" shouts Claire Bowler, not to be outdone.

Strains of a romantic love song drift over from the karaoke run by Jude, Megan and Den while Roz's voice shouts out, "Who'll give me five pounds for three hours babysitting?" She's selling a list of promises she's been collecting all week. "We've already made over a hundred pounds!" she calls to me triumphantly.

A crowd of people is gathered round Brains' stall as he demonstrates his famous Lazy Person's Automatic Nose-picker. (And they're so impressed, they're struck dumb at the sight of it.)

Over by the empty sandpit the toddlers are having their parade, led by Lulu. They're carrying buckets and spades and each of them is wearing a sign with a big letter printed on it. When you join all the letters together it reads:

"GIVE US SOME SAND!"

All the mums and dads are looking on proudly, especially my mum. She's going round with a bucket collecting money to buy sand for the empty pit.

No doubt about it, the fundraiser is a big success.

And, before you know it, it's time

for the best part of all...

The Bike Rally.

The famous Saturday Club Bike Rally that I've been planning forever.

Holy pedal power, how can I do it without my bike!?

The awful thing is, I've been collecting sponsors all week and I can't let them down. (Some people have donated as much as a pound a point and they'll want their moneys' worth.)

There are ten points on the course and you lose one if you hit a bin, fall off a ramp or go inside the perimeters. Of course the biggest point score is for tricks and stunts. (That's why I've been practising wheelies and bunny hops all week.) I *must* do it.

If only I could find my bike.

But Billy is nowhere to be seen. Both my bike and my brother have disappeared. (He knows what's good for him!)

There's nothing else for it...

"Are you sure about this, Max?" Izzie says doubtfully.

I shrug. "Better make the announcement before I change my mind." Izzie knows I hate being laughed at, but maybe what I'm about to do will get people laughing *with* me, instead of *at* me.

Izzie gives a roll on the dustbin drums. "And our next contestant is... Max Boyd... Come on Big Max!"

"Hooray!"

I ride out amidst cheers and laughter, my arms punching the air like a victorious boxer. On to the course I go, my front wheel in the air. Round the bins I speed, faster,

faster, up the ramp, along the plank, wobbling only a little.

The crowd goes mad clapping and cheering and laughing because with this bike I can circle and manoeuvre better than any of them. Wheelies, bunny hops, slaloms, even pivot spins... I do them all in quick succession, weaving and spinning, zoom, zoom, zoom!

On this bike I can do anything.

And as a massive cheer goes up, there's no doubt about it...

On Lulu's little pink bike with the silver fairy bell, I am the winner of the Bike Rally!

13

FINALE

Our steel band can only be a success after that.

And it looks like it will be.

Crowds of people gather round

the paddling pool, spreading out on the grass to the trees beyond. Even Steve is there with the *Big Rock Times* photographer to get a picture for the paper.

"Welcome to the finale of our fundraiser!" announces Roz. "The Saturday Club's very own steel band!"

"HOORAY!"

Izzie, Jen, Brains, Baz, Kala and I run into the centre of the crowd while everybody cheers and claps.

Then the cheering dies down to absolute silence. And in the silent sunshine we begin our finale...

Very softly, very gently, the six of us tap the metal lids with sticks, making a rumbling sound, low yet powerful. The sound gradually increases in intensity until it's a great clanging. Then we pick up the lids and bash them in time together like cymbals. CRASH, CRASH, CRASH!

You should hear it!

Without skipping a beat, we move on to the upturned dustbins. We do these lovely sort of conversation bits where I go *bom... BOM b-bom-bom* and Kala answers back, *tap tappity BANG*. Baz, Brains and Izzie answer with their drumbeats and Jen adds hers. It's a lovely build-up to all of us beating our drums in time together.

My Jamaican grandpa would be proud!

The crowd goes wild, clapping in time to the beat and stomping their feet. Then people get up and start dancing. The whole place is like a giant outdoor rock festival. There's my dad waving his arms and Roz

leaping about. Mum is twirling
round Lulu and Izzie's parents are
jiving. Even Mr Patak is doing a little
wiggle. Everyone's joining in.

*It couldn't be a better finale to
our wonderful fundraiser.*

14

COMMUNITY SERVICE

"Pass me that hammer Max." Dad is nailing together two giant pieces of wood.

I pass Dad the hammer and carry

on with my sanding of a very large pole. When I've got it all nice and smooth I'll feed a giant chain through the holes either end, then suspend it between four shorter posts. (Great for balancing and swinging from!)

We are making the playground equipment.

Izzie and Jen are varnishing the playhouse and Brains is working with my dad's partner, Dave, who's screwing a row of handles into a pole. Sue and Rob are here too, helping with the joints for a huge slatted-wood bridge. It's what you call a joint effort (ha, ha!).

This is going to be one terrific playground.

With Izzie's work getting input from all the kids of Big Rock, we're making the kind of equipment everybody wants.

There are tyres suspended by chains, a sloping rope net to climb over and a row of tunnels to crawl through. So Simon Bowler got his assault course.

And the council is making a huge basketball court for us bigger kids as well as a sloping course for roller blading and bike riding. They're really on our side now.

Building a playground is our way of working together with them. When our parents got letters from Hairy Nose Graham about doing Community Work to pay for stealing the dustbins, it seemed like the obvious thing to do.

Hairy Nose Graham isn't popular with anyone these days. Steve's article exposing his dirty dealings with Betta Industries incensed the good citizens of Big Rock. The headlines were brilliant: "Saturday Club exposes corrupt councillor". The best bit was my quote about discovering Hairy Nose was a big shareholder in Betta. People were scandalized that a young innocent like me should uncover such corruption. I became a star overnight.

The rumour is that Hairy Nose Graham is moving to another town. And I don't think he will be voted to serve as a councillor there...

As for Betta Industries – they lost the bid to build a new supermarket anywhere near Big Rock. Freshfoods are building one instead on the wasteland behind the council offices (the council doesn't need it for old bins any more, **'cos** they've all been recycled).

Funny thing about dustbins.

Despite all the stink Hairy Nose and Betta Industries caused, the wheelie bins are dead popular with the locals in Big Rock now. (Things like new rubbish bins impress people for some reason.) Apparently, even grannies like them because it's easy to *'just tip 'em up and push 'em'* as those men said on that memorable day of the secret delivery.

"How about a mermaid?" Baz is painting the inside of the paddling pool with fish, rocks and underwater sea creatures, including a giant octopus.

"Yes!" says Billy trying not to jump up and down with excitement. He's helping Baz mix colours and he couldn't be happier.

Mind you, I warned him I'm

keeping my eye on him. I said this is just a trial to prove he can be a real human being instead of an aggravating little terror.

It was Izzie's idea to let Billy in on transforming the playground. She reckoned putting him to work would stop his silly tricks and so far I have to admit she's right. (Though I believe the huge argument we had, plus the fact that he had to lay low and miss the fundraiser, had a lot to do with it.)

But that's not the whole story.

The truth is, like the latest litter of white mice... Billy is finally growing up. (And about time too!)

Next year he will be old enough to join the club, and all I can say is he'd better grow up plenty between now and then.

"Hey, see if these handles will

hold you," says Brains who's just finished the handles for a big pole which goes from the playhouse to the top of the steps.

I jump up and hang on to the handle, then I swing from one to the other like a monkey in the trees. "IT'S TERRIFIC!" I shout, swinging on to the newly built playhouse, and standing up. This is just the kind of playhouse our gang imagined when we talked of building a treehouse way back in the autumn.

Standing up there, overlooking the Big Rock Park with all the building going on, I feel dead proud and happy.

Our Saturday Club sits there in the trees and Big Rock Park stretches out below me. We had a battle and we won it.

Yes, Big Rock Park's been taken
over all right...
By the Saturday Club!

1

IT BELONGS TO US

Four measly swings, a horse who's
off his rocker, and a dead duck!
This is the only place the kids of
Big Rock Park have to meet.
So Izzie, Max, Brains and Jen
decide to change things and what
better place for a Saturday
clubhouse than the disused cafe
in the park. But the gang are not
sure the council will be as keen so
they hold a protest – a protest to
save the Saturday Club!

3

CARNIVAL TIME!

It's Carnival Time in Big Rock
and it's hot hot hot! Street parties,
crowds, crazy costumes and best of
all, the Big Rock Carnival Parade.
Can the Saturday Club win
first prize with their amazing
decorated float? Jen reckons
the prize is theirs, but an old
enemy has other ideas...

4

THE MONSTER TRAIL

Is Deep Valley haunted?
Are the terrifying tales of a
Monster from the Deep fact or
fantasy? "The truth is out there,"
Brains says. And he says it so often
the gang decides it's time to track
down the monster. But on the
Saturday Club camping trip to Lake
Deep, Brains' Monster Exposure Kit
unearths more than anyone could
ever have imagined.